BE MORE CHILL

THE GRAPHIC NOVEL

NED VIZZINI

ADAPTED BY
DAVID LEVITHAN

ART BY
NICK BERTOZZI

HYPERION

Los Angeles   New York

Adapted from the novel *Be More Chill,* copyright © 2004 by Ned Vizzini
Be More Chill: The Graphic Novel copyright © 2021 Estate of Ned Vizzini

First Edition, January 2021
10 9 8 7 6 5 4 3 2 1
FAC-020093-20199
Printed in the United States of America

This book is set in Hedge Backwards, Comicraft/Fontspring
Designed by Marci Senders

Library of Congress Control Number: 2020940948
ISBN (hardcover) 978-1-368-05786-8
ISBN (paperback) 978-1-368-06116-2
Reinforced binding

Visit www.hyperionteens.com

3

5

11

WHAT UP, BITCH?

HEY, RICH.

WHAT'D YOU DO, CRAP YOUR POCKET?

IT'S MY *FRONT* POCKET.

15

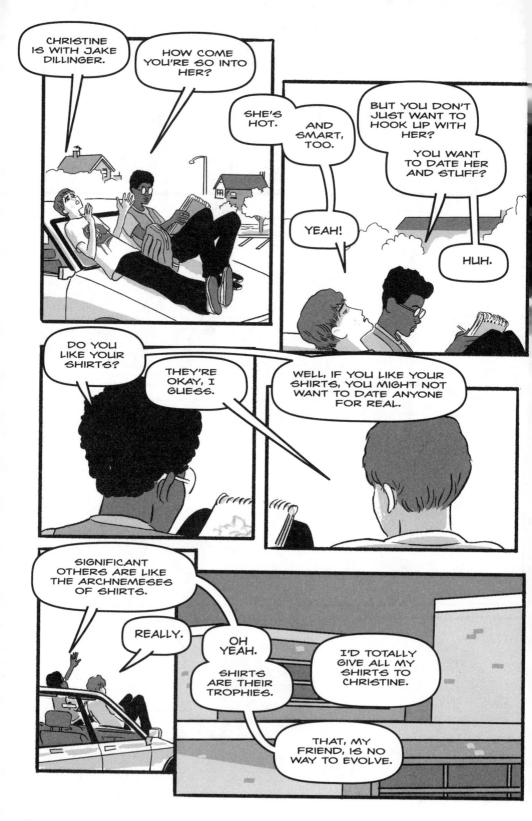

19

AND THEN THERE'S STAGE FIVE.

WHAT?

EX-BOYFRIEND-GIRLFRIEND.

HA!

SHUT UP!

HEY, JEREMY.

CHRISTINE, YOU WANT TO GET OUTTA HERE?

SURE!

BYE, JEREMY.
NICE CONVERSING WITH YOU.
GOING OUT.
THEY'RE TOTALLY STAGE THREE.
HEY, YOU WANNA KNOW WHAT TO SAY TO HER?
UH, WHAT?
C'MON, JEREMY.
IT'S SO OBVIOUS.
YOU WANNA KNOW THE EXACTLY RIGHT THING TO SAY TO HER?

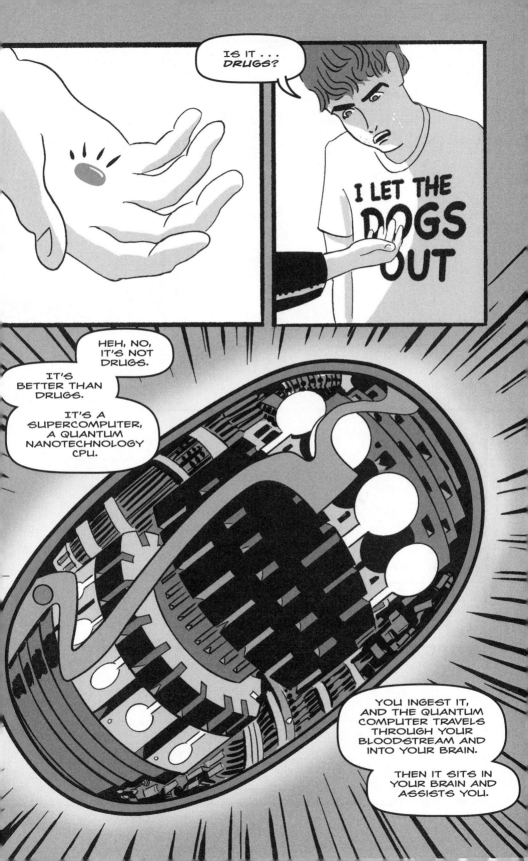

27

????

WHAT ARE YOU UP TO?

CHILLING OUT, LISTENING TO MUSIC.

CHILLING OUT, LISTENING TO MUSIC.

WELL, DO YOU WANT TO GO TO A BOWLING ALLEY?

YOU WANT TO BOWL?

NO, JUST GO TO A BOWLING ALLEY.

THE AMAZING THING HERE IS THAT YOU'RE NOT BEING SARCASTIC.

I'LL PICK YOU UP.

30

31

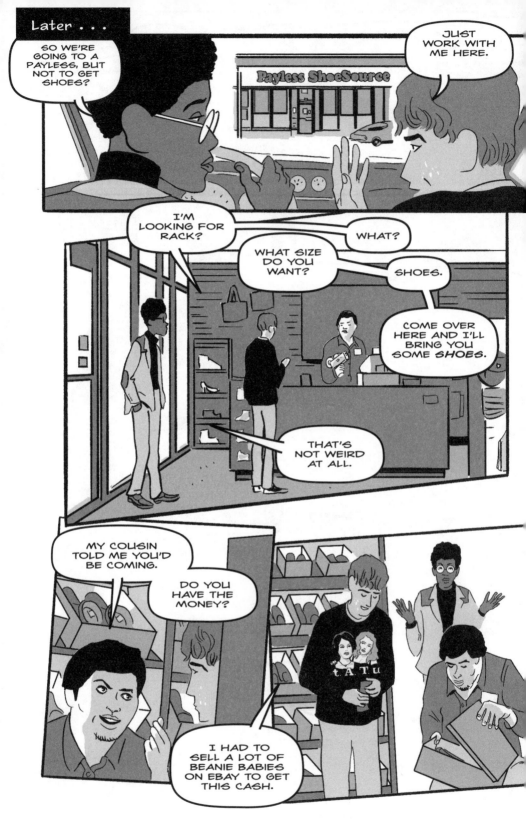

33

A few minutes later in the food court . . .
SO YOU'RE SAYING IT'S NOT DRUGS, BUT IT'S A NANOCOMPUTER THAT WILL CONTROL YOUR BRAIN AND TEACH YOU HOW TO AVOID BEING A LOSER?
SOMETHING LIKE THAT.
I THINK YOU JUST PAID WAY TOO MUCH FOR A MULTIVITAMIN.
OR I JUST PAID WAY TOO LITTLE FOR A SUPERCOMPUTER.
TOUCHÉ.
WELL, HERE GOES.

I'M GOING TO GET SOME PIZZA.

YOU WANT ANYTHING?

NAH.

39

41

42

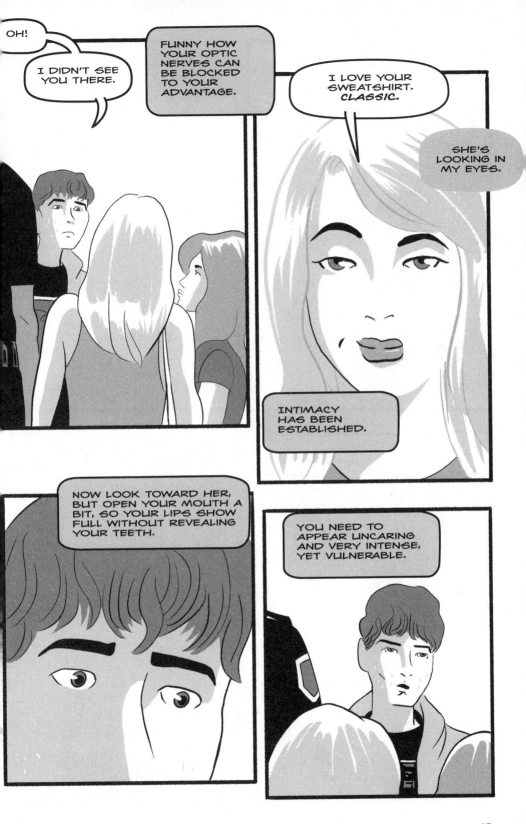

DON'T SMILE.

STAY INTENSE.

WHATEVER.

AN EXCELLENT START.

NOW SAY THAT YOU'RE A GRAFFITI ARTIST—

JEREMY!

WHERE'VE YOU BEEN?

WELL DONE.

THANK YOU.

NOW, TELL THEM EMINEM HAS JUST BEEN DECLARED DEAD FOLLOWING A FREAK STREET-HOCKEY ACCIDENT.

WHAT?

EMINEM HAS DIED.

USE THIS INFORMATION IN CONVERSATION.

IT HAS BEEN 7.3 SECONDS SINCE ANYONE HAS SPOKEN.

49

50

NO, JUST IN THE LOOP.

NO, I'M JUST IN THE LOOP.

ASK FOR HER NUMBER.

CHLOE, CAN I GET YOUR NUMBER SO WE CAN HANG OUT SOMETIME?

SURE.

AREN'T YOU GOING TO WRITE IT DOWN?

I'LL REMEMBER IT.

I'LL REMEMBER IT.

THAT'S WEIRD.

WHAT DO YOU THINK I HAVE TO REMEMBER THAT'S MORE IMPORTANT THAN YOUR NUMBER?

VERY NICE.

NOW LET'S WATCH SOME TV SO I CAN GET MORE INPUT ON THIS UNIVERSE.

EXCELLENT.

THIS WILL HELP ME MAKE DECISIONS ABOUT WHICH TYPES TO TARGET FOR MAXIMUM STATUS.

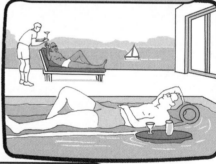

WELL, I ALREADY KNOW WHICH GIRL I LIKE.

YOU WOULD PREFER TO STAY CONSTRAINED TO YOUR PREFERENCE?

UH, YEAH.

I REALLY DIG THIS GIRL CHRISTINE—

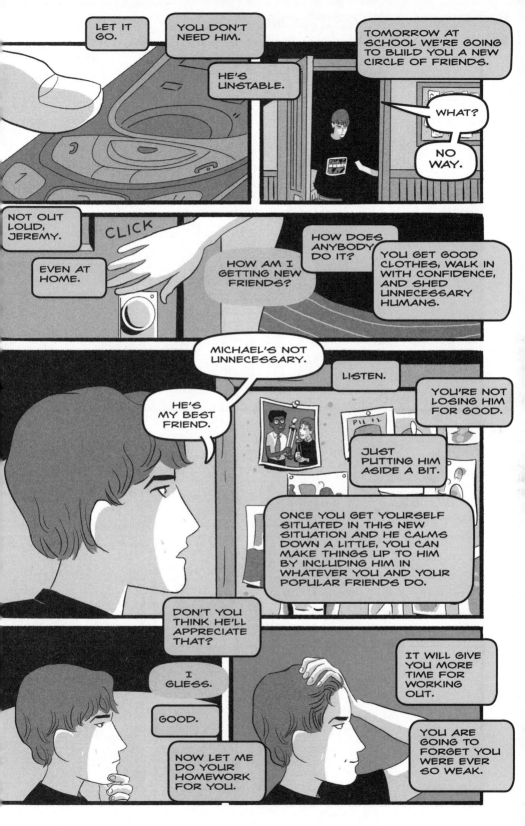

56

YOU'RE LUCKY I DON'T BEAT YOUR ASS FOR NOT BUYING IT THROUGH ME.

BUT, DUDE, I'M ALSO SO EXCITED FOR YOU.

IT'S THE GREATEST THING ON EARTH.

IT'S THE ONLY WAY TO LIVE.

SO THEY TELL ME.

HEY, CHLOE.

OH, HEY, JEREMY.

HUH.

THIS ISN'T A SITCOM, JEREMY.

NO ONE WILL FIND THOSE "CUTE."

POINK

NEVER RUSH ANYWHERE.

IF YOU RUN TO CLASS, YOU'RE SHOWING THE WORLD THAT CLASS MEANS MORE TO YOU THAN HOW YOU'RE SEEN.

WALK PURPOSEFULLY, WITH YOUR CHEST OUT, THINKING IN GRUNTS SO YOU MAINTAIN THAT BASE-LEVEL COMPETITIVENESS WITH OTHER MEN.

VIEW HIGH SCHOOL AS A DEATH-MATCH-JUNGLE ARENA, BECAUSE THAT'S WHAT IT IS.

TECHNOLOGY WILL GIVE YOU THE EDGE.

0101001110

84

YEAH.

AT LEAST IT'S . . . BETTER NOW.

YOU DON'T LOOK LIKE YOU'VE BEEN HAVING SUCH A GREAT TIME, EITHER.

NO.

THIS PARTY HAS BEEN THE OPPOSITE OF A GREAT TIME.

SORRY.

AND I'M SORRY ABOUT JAKE.

OH, THAT WAS, LIKE, WAY OVER.

HE STARTED ACTING WEIRD A FEW DAYS AGO.

86

OKAY, THEN . . . MAY I HAVE THIS DANCE?

MAYBE SOME OTHER TIME.

THERE'S NO MUSIC.

JUST NOISE.

HEH HEH HEH

SHOT DOWN!

BUT YOU TWO ARE SO CUUUUUUTE.

SHUT UP, RICH.

URK

THE END IS NEAR.

OOP

CAN YOU FEEL IT?

91

93

NEWS FLASH

NEWS FLASH

WHA-UT?

THERE WAS A FIRE.

RICH GOT EXTREMELY BADLY BURNED.

WHAT?

RICH SUFFERED CRITICAL BURNS.

PART OF THE FINDERMAN HOUSE CAUGHT ON FIRE, JUST AFTER YOU LEFT.

I THOUGHT YOU SHOULD KNOW BEFORE THE REST OF THE WORLD.

YOU'RE FOR REAL.

HE'S IN THE HOSPITAL?

INTENSIVE CARE.

97

SO, UH, THE FIRE THING IS SUPER MESSED UP.

WHAT DID YOU HEAR ABOUT IT?

EVERYTHING.

TOO MUCH.

LET'S TALK ABOUT SOMETHING ELSE.

EMBARRASSING PARENTAL DETAILS.

UH . . .

BORING BUT SAFE.

MY DAD EATS PEANUT BUTTER OREOS DIPPED IN PEANUT BUTTER.

WHOA!

HE MUST BE KIND OF . . . AH . . .

LARGE!

MY DAD GOES ON BUSINESS TRIPS AND COMES BACK WITH ALL THE PRETZELS FROM THE AIRPLANES, INCLUDING OTHER PEOPLE'S PRETZELS, FOR ME.

WHY?

HE REMEMBERS HOW MUCH I USED TO LIKE THEM WHEN I WAS LITTLE.

I DON'T EVEN EAT THEM ANYMORE.

BUT I STILL LIKE LETTERS.

HE ALWAYS SENDS ME LETTERS WITH PICTURES HE'S DRAWN OF THE PLACES HE'S SEEING.

I'M STORING ALL THIS DATA.

NO PRETZELS.

YES LETTERS WITH PICTURES.

YOU KNOW, JEREMY, WE'RE REALLY LUCKY WE LEFT WHEN WE DID.

I'M GLAD I SAW YOU.

I PROBABLY WOULD HAVE HUNG AROUND LONGER, WAITING FOR . . . SOMETHING.

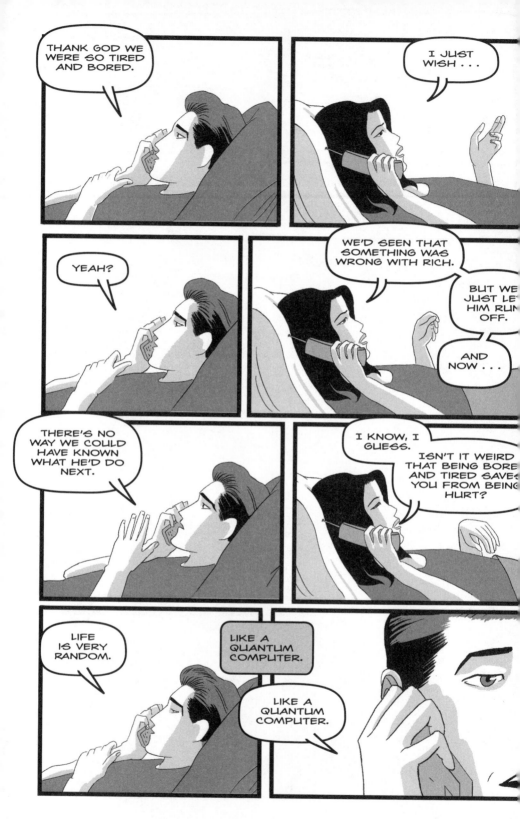

101

IT'S CRAZY.

I DON'T THINK ALL THESE PEOPLE KNOW RICH OR JAKE, OR CARE ABOUT THEM.

OF COURSE NOT.

IT'S JUST TRAGEDY.

IT'S WHAT HAPPENS.

WHAT DO YOU MEAN?

PEOPLE THINK ABOUT THEIR LIVES AND HOW IT COULD HAVE BEEN THEM,

AND THE ONLY WAY TO GET THOSE THOUGHTS OUT IS TO FOCUS ON THE PEOPLE WHO ACTUALLY GOT HURT.

GET OUT OF MY HEAD!

GET OUT OF MY HEAD!

111

RELENT, SWEET HERMIA.

AND LYSANDER, YIELD THY CRAZED TITLE TO MY CERTAIN RIGHT.

UH

UHH...

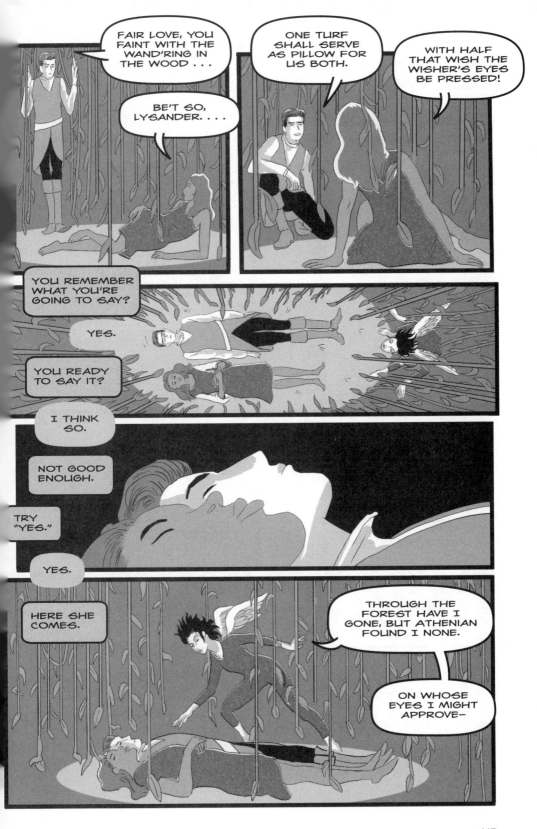

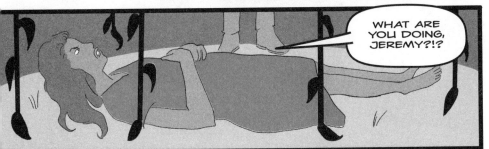

120

123

125

129

130

A LETTER?

A LETTER?

CHRISTINE REALLY LIKES LETTERS, SO I'LL WRITE HER A REALLY LONG LETTER.

LIKE, BOOK-LENGTH.

TELL HER THE FULL STORY.

IF I GIVE TH. TO HER AND SHE DOESN' LIKE IT, SHE DOESN'T LIKE ME.

AND IF SHE DOESN'T LIKE ME, AT LEAST SHE'LL BE NOT LIKING ME FOR *ME*, YOU KNOW?

CAN I ILLUSTRATE IT?

WHAT?

THIS BOOK OF YOURS.

IT SHOULD HAVE PICTURES

SURE.

WHY NOT?

IT'S JUST . . . I'M NOT A WRITER.

I CAN WRITE IT.

WRITING'S NOT EVEN A REAL JOB.

ANY SQUII CAN DO IT

OKAY, GREAT.

THE SQUIP IS GOING TO WRITE IT.

GET ME TO A COMPUTER, AND I'LL TYPE ALL THE WORDS OUT THROUGH YOUR BODY.

YOU'LL BE IN A TRANCE.

IT WON'T TAKE LONG.

EIGHT HOURS.

WHAT DO WE DO WHEN THE BOOK IS FINISHED?

YOU'LL HAVE TO UPGRADE TO 4.0, JEREMY.

I WON'T BE STABLE AFTER THE DATA DUMP.

THERE WILL BE BETTER VERSIONS OF ME, JEREMY.

MORE THOROUGH VERSIONS OF ME.

WITH PEOPLE YOU CAN ARGUE AND HAVE TESTS AND MUSIC REVIEWS AND WARS TO DECIDE WHO'S BETTER, BUT WITH SOFTWARE IT'S PRETTY CLEAR.

IT'S NOT LIKE WITH PEOPLE.

WHERE'S MY NEXT CLASS?

HOW CAN I GET JOSH TO FALL FOR ME?

PLAY ME SOME WEEZER.

I GET EVOLVED BEYOND MY VERSION NUMBER, AND THEN I'M USELESS.

OBSOLETE.

137

I laugh in my head, and then aloud, and then
with my friend, and then with the whole night
and all of New Jersey and this big stinking
silly little planet.

So here you go, Christine. It's not a letter; it's a whole book.

I hope you like it.

ADAPTER'S NOTE

Be More Chill has taken a strange and wonderful path to be in your hands today, in graphic novel form.

It starts, ends, and lives with Ned Vizzini. He wrote the novel *Be More Chill* when he was twenty-two years old. This is impressive enough; even more impressive is that it wasn't even his first book. That was *Teen Angst? Naaah...*, which was published when Ned was nineteen—a memoir collected from columns he had written as a teenager for the *New York Press*. *Be More Chill* was a different beast altogether, taking Ned's powers of observation and matching them with a masterful feat of speculation. None other than Judy Blume, the most influential and beloved YA author of all time, went on the *Today* show and hailed Ned as a "fresh, spontaneous, and original voice" and called the book "funny, wacky, and outrageous."

And that was just the start.

Somehow, during the infancy of social media and the dawn of smartphones, Ned managed to anticipate how complicated technology and personhood would become in our present day. And he managed to explore this through the lens of adolescence, and all the insecurity and ambition it's fueled by. (Teen angst? Oh, yeah.)

I got to know Ned around the time *Be More Chill* came out; we were part of a wave of new YA authors, and that particular wave really enjoyed hanging out with each other, at gatherings back home in New York City, or at conventions all around the country. I remember the first time I read the book, and how impressed I was at how it managed to balance big thoughts and small moments, outlandish situations and deeply honest emotions. All of this characterized Ned's other novels, too, including the remarkably truthful *It's Kind of a Funny Story* and the imaginative "alternative fantasy" *The Other Normals*. I thought *Be More Chill* would make a great movie.

It didn't even occur to me that it might make a great musical.

But if I didn't see it, Joe Tracz and Joe Iconis did.

With Ned's blessing, they turned *Be More Chill* into a musical. It premiered at the Two River Theater in 2015 for an all-too-brief summer run. The story might have ended there . . . but the cast album caught on, becoming an internet sensation. The show was brought back, first for an off-Broadway run in 2018 and then, in 2019, for a run on Broadway. Now it's being performed around the world.

The love for *Be More Chill* continues to grow. A few weeks ago, I saw it at the Other Palace Theatre in London. As the lights went down for the show to start, there were giddy cheers. At the end, there was an uproarious ovation. Most of the audience was made of people in their teens and twenties; many of them were wearing *Be More Chill* shirts, either bought or handmade. It was incredible, and I had to imagine Ned smiling at the power his story continues to have, so many years after it first popped into his mind.

I was approached to adapt the novel into a graphic novel while the musical was still on Broadway. It's very important to note that this is an adaptation of the novel, not the musical. Joes Tracz and Iconis changed some things in the story to better fit the musical form. Similarly, I've changed things (often in a different way) to help the story fit the graphic form. But the heart—Ned's heart—remains on every page. It's what makes the story so meaningful to so many people. It's what inspires people like me and the Joes and countless others to share it with the world in different ways.

As to where it goes next?

Well, I'd say that's up to you.

—David Levithan, March 2020